A Spooky Tale of Spring, Or, How the Grumpy Mom Got her Cheer Back

By Julia Douthwaite Viglione

Illustrations by Kiera Highsmith

With historical and contextual notes by
Chris VandenBossche and Wendy A. Wolfe

Honey Girl
Books and Gifts

Preface

I have endeavored in this scary little book to raise
the Ghost of an Idea, which shall chill you, reader,
for a good cause. May my tale haunt your houses
pleasantly.

Your faithful friend,
J.D.V.

Chapter One
The Ghost of Iris

Iris was dead, to begin with. There is no doubt about that. Mrs. Jones knew because she was out in the backyard just then, stomping down the dirt on top of the little cat's grave. She sighed as she stood up, brushing the dirt off her hands and looking down at the ground.

Yes, Iris was dead as a door-nail.

"That's it with pets," said Mrs. Jones gloomily, "I've had it!"

As she shook off her muddy gloves and walked toward the house, she began mulling over the things to do that weekend. She should take off the storm windows and put up the screens, change the beds, do the laundry, rake up the leaves and clean all the other stuff that had piled up around the house during the long winter.

Ugh.

"Hello there!" cried a cheerful voice, "Isn't it a beautiful day?!" It was the voice of her neighbor, a friendly-looking older man, who stood up from his flower beds to wave at her with a trowel.

"What's so good about it?" she grumbled.

"Why, look at that blue sky," replied the man's voice. "And listen to the birds singing! Spring starts in less than a week."

"That might be fun for you," she returned sternly, "But it's just more work for me." "C'mon now. Don't be a Debby downer," he replied softly. "Even if Tommy's with his dad half-time, you two can still have picnics and play catch in the yard, when it's your turn."

Mrs. Jones turned her head away quickly and sniffed. "Don't tell me how to live. I'm doing just fine," she said. The sun bore down brightly on the quiet yard outside, but everything was dark in her eyes.

"Well, I'm going to the store later on, soon as I get these flowers planted," her neighbor continued. "I hear there might be some shortages coming, with that weird virus afoot. Need anything?"

"No," she said as she turned away.

As she went downstairs to the basement, she heard the happy shouts of children riding bicycles down the street. "Some people never have to work," she muttered to herself.

She heaved up the heavy vacuum and shoved it hard across the thick carpet.

"Get down!" she shouted at the dog who was curled up—in flagrant disobedience—on the white silk couch. Watching the dog hair and dust motes floating in the air, she grumbled, "Think you shed enough? I should never have let Tommy talk me into getting you," she glowered. "All you do is make more work for me. Look at my all my gorgeous stuff; everything ruined by dog hair." (Her living room looked like a *Home Beautiful* photo in gleaming silver and chrome, an impression magnified by the grey marble floors and white rug.)

Marylou, a 12-year-old mutt who usually stuck close to Tommy, looked up apprehensively and cringed. Mrs. Jones smacked her on the rump and shouted, "Down!" Marylou whimpered slightly; her old bones creaked with arthritis and her right leg limped. Looking up at Mrs. Jones with sad brown eyes, she sighed and lumbered off slowly out of sight.

Mrs. Jones cleaned and scrubbed intensely for two hours straight, just as she'd planned. "You slob," she berated herself, "Stop living in a pigsty."

With a stiff back and bleach-smelling hands, she finally sat down, smoothed her hair, and sighed with contentment. "Finally!" she thought, "A chance to do my real work!" Sitting at the long dining table, she looked with pride at the three laptops and two cellphones waiting to serve. It was a dream job, a hard-won position at U_Heep.com, the premier online payday lender.

Although her shoulders tensed at the idea of her vigilant employer and his state-of-the-art surveillance techniques, and she wondered what he would think of all the time she'd just wasted on domestic chores, she logged in. When the U_Heep.com site opened up, she felt a fleeting sensation of joy, just as she did every day upon realizing that she'd made it. She'd arrived.

And now she had access to people's secret financial information from all around the country.

But what was this? The complicated charts were pointing down in utter chaos! Clicking around anxiously from one website to another, all she saw was dismal: her finances were plummeting as, more terrifying, were those of her clients. "Oh my God!" she gasped, "What is going on?" On news sites, she found accounts of a strange virus coming their way, amid forecasts for a world-wide recession, and grim projections of homelessness, starvation, and distress.

Wrapped up in worry, she forgot all about the dog. She didn't take her for a walk or even let her out to do business. She didn't give her dinner or fill her water dish, let alone a treat or a little pat on the head.

Instead, Mrs. Jones sat alone at the table, glued to her bluish screens, and scowled at the world. The dog came by a couple times, whining softly and hoping to be remembered. The first time, Mrs. Jones pushed her aside with her knee. The second time, she shouted at her, "Get lost!" and raised her arm as if to hit her.

So the dog slunk off and curled up quietly by the kitchen door.

Meanwhile, Mrs. Jones ate a melancholy dinner of cheese and crackers, and drank half a bottle of wine, her eyes riveted to the computer screens. At 11:30, she sighed, "That's enough." Closing the computers, she pocketed the phones, locked the front door, went upstairs, and put on her nightgown. After plugging the phones into their holders on the bedside table, she glanced out the window at Iris's fresh grave down below. It looked different somehow. "Shoot," she frowned, "Some animal must have been nosing around in there. Stupid animals. I've had it with pets. Tomorrow, I'm taking that dog to the pound. She's outlived her welcome here anyway."

As she slid down against the pillow, her glance happened to rest upon an alarm clock on her table, behind the phones. She had meant to throw away that old relic. But now, it was with great astonishment and with a strange, inexplicable dread, that she saw the hands of the clock start to turn. They turned so slowly at first that they scarcely made a sound, but as they sped up, they made a shuffling like moth wings flapping against a screen. She got up quickly and went down the hall. She checked Tommy's room, then the guest room, the bathrooms, and all the other rooms. Every single clock was doing the same thing. Digital clocks were flashing bright green and red, their numbers flickering by in a frenzy. The old-fashioned brass clock on her bedside table was spinning its arms so fast she thought they would fly off. Even her cellphones were going crazy! One was flicking numbers so quickly that its screen went blank, while the other one blinked frantically, saying, "ERROR."

This might have lasted half a minute, or a minute, but it seemed an hour. Then the clocks stopped spinning and clicking as they had begun, together.

They were succeeded by a scratching noise, deep down below, as if some huge beast were sharpening its claws on the rug. Mrs. Jones remembered that ghosts in haunted houses were sometimes described as big black cats with long, sharp claws, and she shuddered.

The front door slammed shut with a booming sound, then the noise grew much louder. It started coming up the stairs. It was coming closer. She jumped up, scurried to the bedroom door and locked it.

"Forget it!" she said to herself as she shuffled quickly back to bed, "It's nothing."

Her color changed though, when, without a pause, a ghostly vision passed right through the door and into her room. That same face: the very same except it was much bigger; monstrously huge.

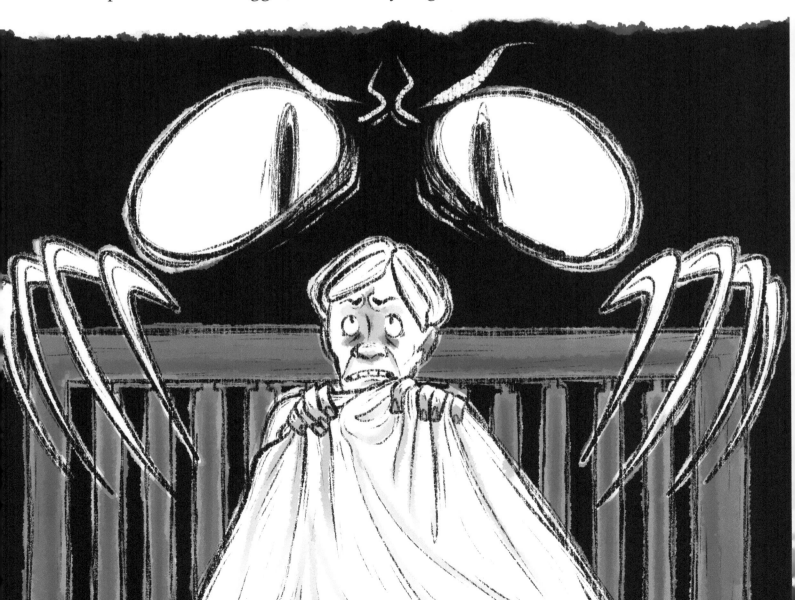

It was Iris, and she had a dead mouse in her mouth, and her claws were bloody red. Her body was transparent, so that as Mrs. Jones looked at her, she could see the bones of other small creatures digesting in her stomach.

Though she looked at the phantom through and through, and saw it crouching on the bed's silken spread; though she felt the chilling influence of its pale gold and green eyes; she was still incredulous and fought against her senses.

"Now what?" asked Mrs. Jones, as caustic and cold as ever. "What do you want with me?"

"Meeeeeeeow!" Iris's voice, no doubt about it. "I want Much!"

"Who are you?"

"Ask me who I was."

"Who *were* you then?" said Mrs. Jones, raising her voice.

"In life I was your cat, Iris." Mrs. Jones looked away.

"You don't believe in me, do you?" observed the ghostly cat.

"No, I do not," said Mrs. Jones.

"Why do you doubt your senses?"

"Because ghosts don't exist. You may be a figment from that last glass of wine, or a bit of undigested apple from my lunch."

The truth is that she was trying to act cool as a means of distracting herself and keeping down the terror, for the specter's voice disturbed the very marrow in her bones.

"Go on," shouted Mrs. Jones, "Scat, cat!"

At this, the spirit raised a frightful cry, picked up the mouse, and shook it back and forth—bumpity, bump, bump, thunk—so many times that Mrs. Jones held on tight to her pillow to save herself from falling into a swoon.

"Good Lord!" she said, "Ghost of Iris, why are you here?"

"Grumpy woman!" replied the Ghost cat, "do you believe in me or not?"

"I guess I do now," murmured Mrs. Jones slowly, "I guess I must. But why do dead pets walk the earth, and why have you come to see me?"

"It is required of every pet," the Ghost cat returned, "That the spirit of their owner shall remain alive in us until they learn to appreciate us, and treat our brethren with love."

"But you never needed much work," faltered Mrs. Jones.

"Work!" screeched the Ghost cat, arching her back, "Work has nothing to do with it. Love was what I sought. And love was what I could have given you. A little pat, a saucer of milk, an occasional caress was all I asked for. In return I would have given you friendship, warm purring, and a soft companion for the night."

The Ghost cat picked up the mouse again and shook the dead carcass, as if that were the cause of her unavailing grief, then she tossed it into the corner.

"You made me scavenge for food, and kill defenseless creatures like this one. You threw me out in the cold, and chased me away when I tried to touch you. Watching you with the old dog tonight," the specter said, "Makes me suffer anew. Why could I not inspire love in you? Why did my companionship not teach you to care for us, your pets?"

Mrs. Jones was very much dismayed to hear the specter going on at this rate, and began to shiver.

"Hear me!" cried the Ghost cat, "My time is nearly gone."

Mrs. Jones pulled the sheets up to her chin, and wiped the sweat from her brow.

"I am here tonight to warn you that you still have a chance and hope of escaping a terrible fate. A chance and a hope that I wish for you, Mrs. Jones."

"You were always a good cat, Iris," said Mrs. Jones, "Thank you."

"You will be haunted," resumed the Ghost cat, "By Two Spirits: one to remind you of the past and one to make you see the present before it is too late."

"Is that the chance and hope you mentioned?" she asked in a faltering voice.

"It is."

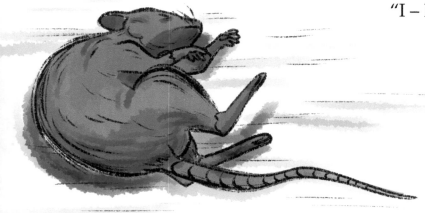

"I – I think I'd rather not," said Mrs. Jones.

"Without their visits," said the Ghost cat, "You cannot hope to mend your ways. Expect the first tomorrow, when the clocks strike one."

"Couldn't I take them both at once and have it over with, Iris?" hinted Mrs. Jones.

"And expect the second one on the next night at the same hour. Look to see me no more; and watch out for your own sake. Mark my words!"

After saying this, the specter leaped off the bed, went to the corner, retrieved the dead mouse with her teeth, and began inching backward toward the window. With every step she took, the window opened a little, so that when the Ghost cat reached it, it was wide open. She beckoned Mrs. Jones to approach. When they were within two paces of each other, the Ghost cat held up a paw, warning her to come no nearer. Mrs. Jones stopped.

She did not stop so much in obedience, as in surprise and fear. For when the phantom raised her paw, Mrs. Jones started hearing weird noises in the air. She heard incoherent sounds of lamentation and regret; moans and barks of cats and dogs that sounded inexpressibly sorrowful and sad. The specter, after listening for a moment, joined in the mournful screeching, and floated out into the bleak, dark night.

Mrs. Jones followed to the window: she felt desperately afraid but terribly curious. She looked out.

The air was filled with phantom pets and mistreated animals. They wandered hither and thither in restless haste, howling, mewing, and whimpering as they went.

Some of them were attached to rusty chains; every one of them had cold dark eyes like the Ghost cat. Ferdinand the bull was there and picadors were shoving spikes into his back. Dumbo the elephant was there too, gazing out blankly from the bars of his cage.

Along with those animals beloved to her through storybooks, many of the others had been personally known to Mrs. Jones in their lives. She saw Fluffy, a bony terrier who had spent many a long hour tied to a post in the neighbors' back yard. She remembered yelling at her when she barked in the night. She saw Whiskers, a skinny cat who nobody seemed to own, and who used to slink through the alley looking for scraps. She recalled throwing a pinecone at him once, and how the cat shrieked and ran away when it hit him in the eye.

Mrs. Jones closed the window, and examined the door by which the Ghost cat had entered. It was locked, as she had locked it with her own hands. She tried to say, "Forget about it," but stopped at the first syllable. And being, from the emotions she had undergone or the fatigues of the day, or the chilling conversation with the Ghost cat, or the lateness of the hour, very tired, she went straight back to bed, and fell asleep upon the instant.

Chapter Two
The First of the Spirits

When Mrs. Jones awoke, it was so dark that she could scarcely distinguish the transparent window from the walls of her room. Looking with her ferret eyes through the gloom, she saw that it was three o'clock. To her great astonishment, the cellphones started blinking, and the minute hand on the old clock started moving again too, clicking faster and faster. Soon it was four o'clock, then five, six, and they went right up to twelve. The clock was wrong; a spring must have broken inside it. (But what about the phones??) It was twelve o'clock!

She lay stunned in the darkness, wondering what was going on, when all of a sudden she remembered that the Ghost had warned her of a visitation that would come at one o'clock. The minutes crept by in rapid succession, and a light flushed up when the bell of the old alarm clock rang ONE. A hand thrust open the curtains, then, and sunshine came flooding into her room.

Mrs. Jones found herself staring up into the face of an unearthly visitor. It was a strange figure—like a child, yet also like an old man, as if it were being seen through some supernatural medium which gave him the appearance of having receded from view and being diminished to a child's proportions. Its hair, which hung about its neck and down its back, was white as if with age, and yet the face had not a wrinkle upon it. A clear jet of light was shining from the top of its head, sparkling like a fountain.

Strangest of all was the black cat that lay curled around its shoulders like a shawl. Upon a command from the creature, the cat stretched, and then hopped up onto his head, extinguishing the light from view.

"Are you the Spirit, sir, whose coming was foretold to me?" asked Mrs. Jones.

"I am."

The voice was soft and gentle. Singularly low, as if instead of being so close beside her, it was far away.

"Who and what are you?" Mrs. Jones asked.

"I am the Spirit of your past."

"Long past?" inquired Mrs. Jones, looking at its dwarfish size.

"Yes and no."

And though Mrs. Jones cowered shyly under the covers, the creature bellowed to her: "Get up! And walk with me now."

Mrs. Jones pleaded that she was only clad in a nightgown and begged for more time. But a cold hand seized her arm. The Spirit pulled her with it and made for the window, like the Ghost cat before. Mrs. Jones became afraid.

"I am a mortal," she said, "And liable to fall."

"Put your hand here," said the Spirit, laying it upon his heart, "And you shall be upheld in more than this!"

As the words were spoken, they rose as if by magic and flew through the walls, above the city streets and into the empty night, until they were over a country road. The lights had entirely vanished. It was a cloudy winter morning; snow was on the ground. A fierce wind was blowing it into drifts.

"Good Heavens!" said Mrs. Jones, "I grew up in this place. I used to play in those fields!"

The Spirit gazed upon her mildly. "Your lip is trembling," said the Ghost.

Mrs. Jones begged the Spirit to lead her where she had to go.

"You remember the way?" inquired the Spirit.

"Remember it!" Mrs. Jones cried in a hoarse voice, "I could walk it blindfolded."

As they followed the road, Mrs. Jones recognized every mailbox, fencepost, and tree. Her grandma's estate lit up the horizon, shimmering grand and imposing behind a snow-covered lawn. But before she could open the wrought iron gate, she heard a whimpering sound. On the other side of the road, about ten feet away, she espied a ramshackle box marked DOGS: FREE. Now and then a small furry head would peek over the box and bark weakly, as the dogs huddled together for warmth.

Just then Mrs. Jones heard angry voices coming from the estate. The front door opened with a bang. "Get that dirty beast out of here!" a woman's voice snarled, "Next time, I'll throw you out too!"

A boy about six years old came shuffling out of the house then, head down, and carrying a small wooden crate. As he crouched to open the lid, Mrs. Jones exclaimed softly, "Jeremy! My little brother! He was always such a sweet little guy."

The door opened again, and she saw more things coming—a hamster cage with a terrified hamster, a fishbowl sloshing its contents, and a ratty-looking dog bed—all of them went flying out the door, before crashing, thumping, and rolling across the snow.

"No more!" shouted the same angry voice. "Pets, you say. Well I call 'em pests, yeah that's right pests."

"Now Dolores," a man's voice murmured from inside, "They're just kids..."

"I told you long ago I never wanted children," she replied icily. "Wish their parents were still here to take care of them, the little slobs...."

A cold wind blew through Mrs. Jones's nightgown and made her shiver. The house, the little boy, and snow-covered hill faded into a greyish haze.

Now the Spirit was leading her through an overgrown garden toward a wooden cottage covered in peeling grey paint. Behind the thin window panes, a cacophony of voices was to be heard: shrieking, howling, and laughing from within.

"Speckles, jump through the hoop," cried a little girl in grubby-looking jeans, while an excited dog wagged its tail. "Polly wants a cracker! Polly wants a cracker! Aack!" screamed a green parrot flying overhead. "Mommy, Mommy look at me," a toddler yelled as he stumbled in, lugging a kitten that was doing its best to squiggle out of a doll dress.

A smiling woman in eyeglasses, with her greying hair in a sloppy ponytail, looked on from the doorway with one arm around a plump little man holding a dishrag. "Such joy they are, these children. I wish these days would never end."

Suddenly the vision imploded; waxy black smoke choked the hallway and orange flames went leaping up the stairs. Footsteps ran and then went silent. The timbers crumbled and fell.

"Spirit!" said Mrs. Jones in a broken voice, "Remove me from this place!"

"These are the shadows of things that have been," said the Ghost. "They are what they are. Do not blame me."

"Please take me back!" Mrs. Jones exclaimed. "I can't stand it anymore."

The Spirit's light was burning high and bright. Mrs. Jones took the black cat off the Spirit's shoulders and put it on its head. The cat curled up, smothering the light and driving the vision from sight. Soon she was home again and there was nothing left but a patch of warmth on the bedroom rug.

Mrs. Jones was conscious of being exhausted and overcome by an irresistible drowsiness. She had barely time to fall into bed before she sank into a heavy sleep.

Chapter Three
The Second Spirit

Awaking in the middle of a loud snore, and sitting up to get her thoughts together, Mrs. Jones remembered with a start what was to happen next. Turning this way and that, she watched apprehensively for the second spirit's arrival.

Now, being prepared for almost anything, she was not by any means prepared for nothing! Consequently, when the minute hand hit twelve and no one appeared, she was taken by a violent fit of trembling. Five minutes, ten minutes, a quarter of an hour came and went by, yet nothing came. Suddenly she noted a ray of reddish light shining in from under the bedroom door, and got up. The moment she put her hand on the doorknob, a strange voice called her by name and bade her come. She opened the door as if in a trance.

The hall was aglow. As she followed the warm light, she had no doubt that it was still her house, but it did not at all look like her house. It had undergone a surprising transformation!

The walls were hung with rosy-colored tapestries and plush velvet quilts that seemed to tell stories. Wood floors scratched by wear replaced the cool marble, and they were covered in bright rugs with flower designs. The stylish white sofas were gone; in their place were oversize brown couches covered with blankets: there were crazy quilts made of children's clothing, and heirloom-looking crocheted covers, fuzzy flannel for cold nights, and light cotton throws in case of a chill. The floor was cluttered with chew toys, yarn balls, and a pair of well-worn slippers; piles of books and magazines sprawled in merry mess.

Asleep in five beds set near the hearth were two dogs and three cats, kept warm by a glorious fire. The air smelled good, like fresh baked bread with a touch of cinnamon, vanilla, and orange zest.

In easy state upon the plush couch, there sat a jolly Giant, glorious to see, who bore a glowing torch and held it up high to shed its light on Mrs. Jones as she came peeping around the door.

"Come in!" exclaimed the Ghost. "Come in and know me better, woman!" Mrs. Jones entered timidly, and hung her head before the Spirit.

"I am the Ghost of the present," said the Giant, "Look upon me!"

He was a huge and lumbering figure that reminded her of the Paul Bunyan statue she'd once seen in a California park. He had grubby jeans and stout brown boots, a light blue work shirt with the sleeves rolled up (revealing an enormous heart-shaped tattoo), and a bright red cap on his head. His fingernails were dirty, his callused hands were huge, and his eyes sparkled brightly.

Mrs. Jones gazed upon him in wonder. "Spirit," she said submissively, "Take me where you will. I went forth last night and I learned a sorry lesson. Tonight, if you have anything to teach me, let me profit from it."

"Grab my shirt!"

Mrs. Jones did as she was told, and held on fast.

Cushions and comforters, slippers and pillows all vanished instantly. So did the room, the fire, the ruddy glow, and the pets. Before you could say "Jack Sprat," they were standing in the middle of a green meadow on a late-spring afternoon. People and dogs were everywhere to be seen. Little children and puppies were drinking water at a spring-fed fountain. Moms and dads were chuckling over the pranks. Grandmas pushing baby carriages went jogging across the sweet-smelling grass just for the joy of movement.

A Jack Russell terrier was nosing through the clover, as big old Dalilah the Saint Bernard went clumping along behind it. Guiness the boxer came running up with a smile to meet his friend Chauncey the black lab. Poodles and basset hounds, wiener dogs and water dogs, all were running and rolling and relishing the good earthy smells of dirt and warm grass.

Mrs. Jones said, "This is all very nice, but we both know that many other dogs are stuck in pens and locked in cages on this very afternoon. Others are abandoned in trash cans, or dumped by the side of the road. Why do you Spirits allow so many animals to suffer?"

"Some people upon this earth of yours," said the Spirit, "Claim that they know me. They do deeds of ill-will, envy, and cruelty in my name. But they are as strange to me and my family as if they had never lived. Remember that, and charge their doings on them, not on us."

Mrs. Jones promised that she would, and they went on, invisible as they had been before, into the outskirts of town.

And perhaps it was the pleasure that the Good Spirit had in showing off his powers, or else it was his generous, hearty nature and his sympathy with poor folk, but for some reason they went straight to Mrs. Jones's brother's house.

On the threshold of the door, the Spirit smiled, and stopped to bless Jeremy Smith's dwelling with sprinklings of his torch. Think of that! Jeremy made but $40,000 a year for his family of five, and yet the Ghost of the Present blessed his house just the same!

Up rose Katrina, Jeremy's wife, dressed in paint-spattered denim like most every day, and three small children, two boys and a girl who came tearing in yelling excitedly about the mac-n-cheese they could smell from outside. Jeremy stomped in next, grinning from ear to ear and knocking the mud from his boots. He left a dirty trail of grit on the floor as he came over to give his wife a peck on the cheek.

"Looks like the little ones will be coming soon!" he exclaimed, referring to the kennel behind the house. "Yay, more puppies!" his kids cheered, and their mom smiled happily, piling dinner on cracked pottery plates.

Then the family drew round the kitchen table, and the daddy proposed a toast, "To Daisy, the best dog in the world and soon-to-be mother of our pups! God bless her, and all of us!"

"God bless us all!" The family echoed.

"I'm so glad that dogs can't catch that scary virus, Daddy," said the little girl shyly. "But where will the puppies live later? Could we give one to Auntie Jones and Tommy?"

"Yeah!" "I bet Marylou would like a pup to keep her company, now that Iris has died," shouted the little boys.

The parents eyed each other warily over the children's heads, and looked down sadly.

"We'll see about that later," they murmured.

By this time, it was getting dark and the sun was setting. Willows shrouded the little house in darkness. The Spirit whisked Mrs. Jones high into the air then. They flew all around the country, and traversed season after season.

Much they saw, and far they went, and many homes they visited, but always with a happy end. When the Spirit landed beside a sick bed, a kitten materialized in his hand. The kitten hopped lightly onto the wan woman's sheet and batted at her bedclothes, making the tired face smile. When the Spirit materialized in jails and homeless shelters, he brought mellow old dogs along. They sat peacefully alongside the people and kept them company during the long hours of solitude. Even where people barred the Spirit out, he left his blessing, and taught Mrs. Jones his generous ways.

It was a long night, if it was only one night. Mrs. Jones had her doubts about that because it seemed like whole lifetimes had been condensed into the time they spent together. It was strange too that, while Mrs. Jones remained the same, the Ghost was growing older before her eyes.

"Are spirits' lives so short?" asked Mrs. Jones.

"My life upon this globe is very brief," replied the Ghost. "It ends tonight." "Tonight!" echoed Mrs. Jones faintly.

"Tonight at midnight. Hark! The time is drawing near."

The chimes of Holy Cross School were ringing three quarters past eleven at that moment.

"Forgive me if I appear indiscreet," said Mrs. Jones looking intently at the Spirit's shirt, "But I see something strange on the back of your shirt. It seems to be a foot or a claw!"

"It could have been a claw, except that there is flesh upon it," was the Spirit's sorrowful reply. "Look here."

From behind his back, he hauled out two children, wretched and abject, and each was holding a pet of equally miserable appearance.

"Oh woman! Look here. Look, look at them."

They were a boy and a girl, holding an old grey dog and a skinny ginger cat. Yellow, meager and scowling, the children were haggard and humble. Where graceful youth should have filled out their features and cast a healthy glow on them, they looked wolfish and cunning. The animals they were holding looked similarly corrupt. It seemed that a shriveled hand, like that of age, had pinched and twisted them and made skinny wretches out of the once-beautiful creatures.

"Spirit! Are they yours?" Mrs. Jones asked in a hushed tone.

"No, they belong to you, all of you humans."

Looking down sorrowfully upon them, the Ghost continued: "They cling to me, since no one else will have them. The boy's name is Ignorance, and his pup is called Hunger. This girl is Want, and her cat's name is Cruelty. Beware of them, and all of their kind, but most of all beware the boy. Written upon his brow I see your Doom, unless the writing can be erased. Admit it, and bide the consequences!"

"Have they no refuge or resources?" asked Mrs. Jones. "I thought online learning was supposed to take care of kids like that. And what about foster homes and pet shelters? It's too much to ask a person like me to help." The bell struck twelve. Mrs. Jones looked about her for the Ghost, and saw it no longer. As the last stroke ceased to vibrate, she remembered the prediction of old Iris, and lifting up her eyes to heaven, sought a sign or an omen to tell her what to do.

Chapter Four
A Bad Night's Sleep

Nothing came. An icy wind blew down the street and swirled around her bare ankles. "Enough," she muttered, as she turned back to the house and went up to bed. But even though she was immensely tired, and tried any number of soothing apps on her phone, sleep was not forthcoming. Around and around her mind went painful thoughts of the past and fearful thoughts of the future. One scenario haunted her: a conversation overheard weeks ago when she was at the office of U_Heep.com. Huddled over the espresso machine, she had heard the company's CEO, Mr. Uriah Heep, Sr., walking by with his son, Mr. Uriah Heep, Jr. who was her boss. They were whispering something about layoffs and furloughs, and Heep Sr. laughed out loud when his son used finger quotes and suggested firing the "liberated women" first. "Haha, very good! Let them eat cake," Heep Sr. had sneered, "In my 'umble opinion, they deserve it."

That vision crushed her again and again. Without the job, she feared, the career she'd built so carefully would screech to a halt, her platinum credit rating would tank, and she'd become a foolish stereotype: a middle-aged divorcee living in an oversize house full of debts.

"That's okay," she mumbled in her sleep, "I can make a living with online betting, or set up a Ponzi scheme, maybe? Surely some of those schmucks at U_Heep.com would follow? I'll get rid of the dog tomorrow, and sign up for my own business license. I'll show them all!"

Then another voice would emerge, warning: "HA! Fine idea in the midst of a pandemic. You're more likely to die alone, you moron." A second vision then became visible: it was a plate of half-eaten cheese and crackers sitting on a dining table by a wineglass, surrounded by laptops and cellphones, as a crumpled female figure lay helpless on the floor, gasping for breath and turning blue.

"No! No! No!" she shrieked and sat up abruptly, to find herself alone in bed.

"No! I'll do better!" she said, and grabbing a pad of paper and a pen, she began making a list. "Tomorrow morning I'll get up first thing and call Jeremy. I'll visit Katrina's studio, if she'll let me, and really look at her paintings this time. I'll invite the kids to come here, and maybe even stay for a while. We'll find something to do, we'll do, will do will do," she said as she dropped the pen and slipped back into sleep: a nice restorative snooze that lasted til noon.

Chapter Five
The Return of Cheer

When she awoke and peered around, she was still alone. It was still today. She was still alive. "Thank heavens!" she thought. Opening her bedroom door, she found the dog had been sleeping right outside. "Well, hi there, Marylou!" she smiled and stooped over to give her a pat. The dog wagged her tail and lumbered into action, following her mistress down the stairs. As Mrs. Jones looked around, she thought of ways to make the big house cozier. After letting the dog out back, and filling up her food and water bowls, Mrs. Jones glanced out the front door and saw something strange. "What is that?" she wondered with an anxious frown. There was something coming down the path, right toward her house. It was small and white and had a long tail. She thought it was another Ghost and braced herself for more horror. "Well, virus or no virus," she thought, "I've got to see what that thing is," and so she opened the door and headed out.

Imagine her surprise when the phantom turned out to be a white kitten that wound softly around her legs and said a squeaky "Mieeeuw."

"What's your name, little one?" Mrs. Jones wondered aloud, as she bent over to scoop up the tyke. "What's this on your neck?"

As the kitten arched its back and purred, Mrs. Jones could feel its heart beating hard; it was scared but pretending to be brave. She pulled a little piece of notebook paper that was tucked under the cat's collar. It said: "My name is Cheer. Please take me home. If you do, I will love you from now until eternity. I need you. Maybe you need me too."

"Oh kitty," said Mrs. Jones with a choke, "You know I will."

As she slowly walked back into her house, Mrs. Jones saw Marylou sitting in the kitchen, wagging her tail and smiling her goofy smile. Mrs. Jones thought about the Spirits as she moved about the kitchen, giving her new friend a dish of milk, and watching the dog slurp up her water. The dog drank heavily then left a trail of drops across the floor as she went to sniff the newcomer, who saluted her with a flick of the tail, and purred loudly in milky bliss.

"Silly Marylou," Mrs. Jones whispered affectionately, "You want to make friends, don't you?"

Mrs. Jones had no further contact with Spirits, but lived in good cheer and kindliness from then on, despite the terrible virus that was ravaging our world. As the weeks, then months of lockdown continued, the dreaded lay-off letter from U_Heep.com arrived. Yet she did not panic. Instead, she looked within, remembering the lessons of the Spirits, and asked her family for help. They were glad to oblige!

Her brother and sister-in-law taught her how to grow things and how to operate a sewing machine and other household tools. She repaid their kindness with nice meals and books for the kids. With more time on her hands and good books she'd been waiting to read, she became wiser and more patient. She turned her new sewing skills into face masks, then sewed hundreds of them for the homeless and elderly folks in her town. While she never became a great gardener, she did invite the neighbors to dig up her front and back lawns and plant their own family gardens. Soon there were corn stalks and sunflowers waving their arms above tomato plants, carrots, and lavender.

When the virus died down, she found a new job teaching financial literacy classes at a local college and made an adequate income that way: sharing knowledge she once had kept secret. But the thing that made her happiest was her new friends. As the days went by, she got to know the local boys and girls by asking for their help in creating a neighborhood makerspace. They in turn enlisted some moms and dads who were expert in carpentry, and

together the group converted the guest room into an airy workshop where the kids could come after school to create things, just for fun. Soon the whirring sounds of a sewing machine and a 3-D printer could be heard at all hours of the day and night. Passersby would sometimes smell the burnt wood from the laser cutter and make out the eerie buzzing sounds of a drill-press. Once the COVID-19 virus waned and face masks were not so much in demand, the sewing kids began making artwork and quilts—complicated geometric quilts, baby quilts, and crazy jazz-style quilts. Each quilt had a little message stitched in: they spoke of hope, and love, and respect for our world.

Meanwhile, the number of pets in her home grew and grew; old spaniels and wounded sparrows, plush Persians and skinny strays, they all found a way to the Joneses' house. Yet, with Tommy spending more time away, the house seemed a little empty. And it got so dirty. Cat and dog hair piled up in the corners, and wafted about when they walked through the rooms, not

to mention the wood shavings and dust that somehow came down from upstairs. No matter how much she cleaned, it came back: exasperating! But instead of getting mad, Mrs. Jones got creative. She went online and ordered a friendly-looking little robot from a new firm in town. The pets didn't like it, but they learned to move out of the way when it whirred around the rooms vacuuming up the mess on its daily rounds.

Next, she started thinking about more remodeling, and invited her sister-in-law to redesign the den and living room into a painting studio and a gallery to display everybody's creations. They had a hunch people might come by once the lockdown ended. And they were right. Although people were still cautious and wore masks, word soon spread of Katrina's paintings, the gorgeous quilts, and the funny, snarky wooden plaques made by local teenagers. Within weeks the in-house art exhibits became incredibly popular.

Some say the works were magic, because they seemed to bring love and life to all who saw them.

Little by little, people who had once feared Mrs. Jones began changing their minds about her. They dropped by regularly to visit now, instead of rushing by on their walks. They loved looking at the art and crafts, tickling the kittens and playing fetch with the dogs. There was something nice about her place; it always smelled so good! It was the smell of love: cinnamon, peppermint, and vanilla, the yeasty bliss of fresh-baked bread, with a whiff of coffee and just a bit of orange zest, sawdust, and oil paint.

Although it was now far less tidy than it had been before, people said that Mrs. Jones really knew how to keep house. And that she had the biggest heart around.

May that be truly said of us, all of us! And may we all share our lives with a pet.

(With thanks to Charles Dickens, *A Christmas Carol*, 1843)

Historical and Contextual Notes

1. Historical note on Victorian England, the context of *A Christmas Carol*, by Chris VandenBossche

A Christmas Carol appeared in 1843 at an important point in Dickens's career and a key moment in the history of Victorian England. One economic recession in the late 1830s and another in the early 1840s had prompted widespread social unrest. A major working-class movement petitioned the government in 1839 and 1842 to establish universal manhood suffrage (at the time only one in five adult males were qualified to vote and no women could vote). The Reform Bill of 1832 had very slightly increased the number of eligible voters but left out the working classes. Even worse, the Parliament elected after its passage enacted a New Poor Law that made life even harder for the lower classes by requiring that anyone seeking poor relief—what we now call welfare—must live in a workhouse, a sort of voluntary prison where they were fed a rudimentary diet and set to meaningless work. This is what Scrooge refers to when he asks the men seeking donations for the poor if the "workhouses . . . are still in operation" and the "Treadmill and the Poor Law are in full vigour."

The other principle embodied in the law was that individuals are responsible only for themselves. This idea leads Scrooge to dismiss the benevolent men by saying that "It's enough for a man to understand his own business, and not to interfere with other people's." After the visits of the spirits, however, Scrooge's view of the world is transformed when his late business partner Jacob Marley insists that he should have understood that "Mankind was my business. The common welfare was my business; charity, mercy, forbearance, and benevolence, were, all, my business." Rather than imagining a change in the law, Dickens envisions the conversion of Scrooge from a businessman who believes he should only be concerned with his own financial interest into an enlightened employer who feels kinship with and responsibility for his employees and fellow citizens.

2. "Hope" by Wendy A. Wolfe

In the United States, 2019 brought forth a victory for the protection of animals when both the House of Representatives and the Senate passed the PACT (Preventing Animal Cruelty and Torture) Act.* Across the country volunteers have stepped up their efforts to give animals a second chance. In Mishawaka, Indiana, the "Homeward Bound Animal Welfare Group" rescues dogs from breeding facilities and kill shelters. These dogs can be adopted via the Homeward Bound Facebook page or website (below).

During the COVID-19 pandemic, I found myself perusing animal rescue sites and ended up adopting a dog from Homeward Bound Animal Rescue. The process was easy and transformative for both me and my new family member, who I renamed "Hope." My other dogs greeted her well as did my several rescue cats and within just a few days she began changing into a confident and fun-loving little dog. I can't even describe the love this little dog has in her heart that would have gone unknown to me without a second chance. Everyone deserves a second chance and a happy ending, so do yourself a favor and give yourself a second chance at love by rescuing a dog or cat just waiting to fill your heart anew.

*See Emily Ehrhorn, "Extreme animal cruelty can now be prosecuted as a federal crime," *The Humane Society of the United States Press Release*, 25 November 2019. https://www.humanesociety.org/news/extreme-animal-cruelty-can-now-be-prosecuted-federal-crime

50% of the proceeds from *A Spooky Tale of Spring* will be donated to Homeward Bound Pet Rescue organization, Mishawaka, Indiana.

https://www.homewardboundawg.com/

Loved the story?
Want your own Story-telling quilt?

Honey Girl to the rescue! We specialize in cozy.

"Alice in Wonderland" quilt (small size)

"Frankenstein" quilt (small size)

Story-Telling quilts, exclusively at:
https://www.etsy.com/shop/HoneyGirlBooksGifts

CPSIA information can be obtained
at www.ICGtesting.com
Printed in the USA
BVHW020812031221
623155BV00006B/74